Lighthead

Lighthead

Terrance Hayes

PENGUIN POETS

PENGUIN BOOKS
Published by the Penguin Group
Penguin Group (USA) Inc., 375 Hudson Street, New York, New York 10014, U.S.A.
Penguin Group (Canada), 90 Eglinton Avenue East, Suite 700, Toronto, Ontario,
Canada M4P 2Y3 (a division of Pearson Penguin Canada Inc.)
Penguin Books Ltd, 80 Strand, London WC2R 0RL, England
Penguin Ireland, 25 St Stephen's Green, Dublin 2, Ireland
(a division of Penguin Books Ltd)
Penguin Group (Australia), 250 Camberwell Road, Camberwell,
Victoria 3124, Australia (a division of Pearson Australia Group Pty Ltd)
Penguin Books India Pvt Ltd, 11 Community Centre, Panchsheel Park,
New Delhi – 110 017, India
Penguin Group (NZ), 67 Apollo Drive, Rosedale, North Shore 0632, New Zealand
(a division of Pearson New Zealand Ltd)
Penguin Books (South Africa) (Pty) Ltd, 24 Sturdee Avenue, Rosebank,
Johannesburg 2196, South Africa

Penguin Books Ltd, Registered Offices:
80 Strand, London WC2R 0RL, England

First published in Penguin Books 2010

10 9

Copyright © Terrance Hayes, 2010
All rights reserved

Page xi constitutes an extension of this copyright page.

LIBRARY OF CONGRESS CATALOGING IN PUBLICATION DATA
Hayes, Terrance.
Lighthead / Terrance Hayes.
p.   cm.—(Penguin poets)
ISBN 978-0-14-311696-7
I. Title.
PS3558.A8378L54   2010
811'.54—dc22   2009053319

Printed in the United States of America
Set in Avant Garde
Designed by Ginger Legato

For our lit and light blue Love

CONTENTS

ACKNOWLEDGMENTS

My sincere thanks to the editors and staff of the following publications for first acknowledging the poems (and previous versions of the poems) in this manuscript:

American Poetry Review, Bat City Review, Barrelhouse magazine, *Black Warrior Review, Black Renaissance Noire, Callaloo, Columbia Poetry Review, Court Green, Guernica: A Magazine of Art and Politics, Harvard Review, Indiana Review, jubilat, Konundrum Engine Literary Review, McSweeney's Literary Journal, McSweeney's Online, MiPOesias, Muckworks, New Letters, New Orleans Review, Ploughshares, Poetry, Quarterly West, Sou'wester, Smartish Pace, The New Yorker, Third Coast,* and *Washington Review.*

"The Avocado" also appeared in *State of the Union: Fifty Political Poems,* edited by Joshua Beckman and Matthew Zapruder.

"Cocktails with Orpheus" and "Mystic Bounce" also appeared in *Between Water and Song: New Poets for the Twenty-first Century,* edited by Norman Minnick.

"The Elegant Tongue" appeared in *Legitimate Dangers: American Poets of the New Century,* edited by Cate Marvin and Michael Dumanis.

"Fish Head for Katrina" also appeared in *So Much Things to Say! 100 Calabash Poets,* edited by Kwame Dawes.

"A House Is Not a Home" also appeared in *The Best American Poetry 2009,* edited by David Wagoner and David Lehman.

Deepest gratitude to Yona Harvey, Rob Casper, Shara McCallum, Jeffery Thomson, and Crystal Williams for laying their careful eyes on this collection; and to the Guggenheim Foundation for its generous support. Thanks, as well, to those who influenced this manuscript through friendship, encouragement, and conversation: Elizabeth Alexander, Radiclani Clytus, Toi Derricotte, Adrian Matejka, Paul Slovak, and my families.

Lighthead

It is a fire that consumes me, but I am the fire.

—Jorge Luis Borges, "A New Refutation of Time"

LIGHTHEAD'S GUIDE TO THE GALAXY

Ladies and gentlemen, ghosts and children of the state,
I am here because I could never get the hang of Time.
This hour, for example, would be like all the others
were it not for the rain falling through the roof.
I'd better not be too explicit. My night is careless
with itself, troublesome as a woman wearing no bra
in winter. I believe everything is a metaphor for sex.
Lovemaking mimics the act of departure, moonlight
drips from the leaves. You can spend your whole life
doing no more than preparing for life and thinking,
"Is this all there is?" Thus, I am here where poets come
to drink a dark strong poison with tiny shards of ice,
something to loosen my primate tongue and its syllables
of debris. I know all words come from preexisting words
and divide until our pronouncements develop selves.
The small dog barking at the darkness has something to say
about the way we live. I'd rather have what my daddy calls
"skrimp." He says "discrete" and means the street
just out of sight. Not what you see, but what you perceive:
that's poetry. Not the noise, but its rhythm; an arrangement
of derangements; I'll eat you to live: that's poetry.
I wish I glowed like a brown-skinned pregnant woman.
I wish I could weep the way my teacher did as he read us
Molly Bloom's soliloquy of yes. When I kiss my wife,
sometimes I taste her caution. But let's not talk about that.
Maybe Art's only purpose is to preserve the Self.
Sometimes I play a game in which my primitive craft fires
upon an alien ship whose intention is the destruction
of the earth. Other times I fall in love with a word
like *somberness*. Or moonlight juicing naked branches.
All species have a notion of emptiness, and yet

the flowers don't quit opening. I am carrying the whimper
you can hear when the mouth is collapsed, the wisdom
of monkeys. Ask a glass of water why it pities
the rain. Ask the lunatic yard dog why it tolerates the leash.
Brothers and sisters, when you spend your nights
out on a limb, there's a chance you'll fall in your sleep.

[THE LAST TRAIN TO AFRICA]

ALL THE WAY LIVE

"Do all dudes have one big testicle and one little tiny one?"
Hieronymus asked, hiking up his poodle skirt as we staggered
Down Main Street in our getup of wigs and pink bonnets
The night we sprayed NEGROPHOBIA all over the statue of Robert
E. Lee guarding the county courthouse, a symbol of the bondage
We had spent all of our All-the-Way Lives trying to subvert.
Hieronymus's thighs shimmered like the wings of a teenage
Cockroach beneath his skirt as a bullhorn of sheriff verbs
Like *Stop! Freeze!* and *Fire!* outlined us. The town was outraged:
The red-blooded farm boys, the red-eyed bookworms of Harvard,
The housewives and secretaries, even a few liberals hoorayed
When they put us on trial. We were still wearing our lady ward-
Robes, Hieronymus and me, with our rope burns bandaged
And our wigs tilted at the angle of trouble. Everyone was at war
With what it meant to be alive. That's why we refused to be banished,
And why when they set us on fire, there was light at our core.

THE GOLDEN SHOVEL

after Gwendolyn Brooks

I. 1981

When I am so small Da's sock covers my arm, we
cruise at twilight until we find the place the real

men lean, bloodshot and translucent with cool.
His smile is a gold-plated incantation as we

drift by women on bar stools, with nothing left
in them but approachlessness. This is a school

I do not know yet. But the cue sticks mean we
are rubbed by light, smooth as wood, the lurk

of smoke thinned to song. We won't be out late.
Standing in the middle of the street last night we

watched the moonlit lawns and a neighbor strike
his son in the face. A shadow knocked straight.

Da promised to leave me everything: the shovel we
used to bury the dog, the words he loved to sing,

his rusted pistol, his squeaky Bible, his sin.
The boy's sneakers were light on the road. We

watched him run to us looking wounded and thin.
He'd been caught lying or drinking his father's gin.

He'd been defending his ma, trying to be a man. We
stood in the road, and my father talked about jazz,

how sometimes a tune is born of outrage. By June
the boy would be locked upstate. That night we

got down on our knees in my room. *If I should die
before I wake,* Da said to me, *it will be too soon.*

II. 1991

Into the tented city we go, we-
akened by the fire's ethereal

afterglow. Born lost and cool-
er than heartache. What we

know is what we know. The left
hand severed and school-

ed by cleverness. A plate of we-
ekdays cooking. The hour lurk-

ing in the afterglow. A late-
night chant. Into the city we

go. Close your eyes and strike
a blow. Light can be straight-

ened by its shadow. What we
break is what we hold. A sing-

ular blue note. An outcry sin-
ged exiting the throat. We

push until we thin, thin-
king we won't creep back again.

While God licks his kin, we
sing until our blood is jazz,

we swing from June to June.
We sweat to keep from we-

eping. Groomed on a die-
t of hunger, we end too soon.

SHAKUR

I'm coming at you live from the halfway out
Where the winter morning stretches out

Like a white sheet over lovers the infinite
Has fetched. The still and bone-blue white

Couple found parked, frozen on the highway,
I'm thinking of them and the drug that made

Them think they were warm enough to chill
Because I know staying alive requires pills

And a wicked streak. I'd need a head cocooned
In bass, I'd need to be locked in a womb

To hear your dopey two-note melody, your song
Pimped by wreckage, your light longing

For lightness. I'd have to be as quiet
As the youths whose youth made them stupid

And lovely. They are God's niggaz now like you.
I'm thinking of the stall of intoxicated cool

That stalled you before it stalled them. I know
Men who want to die this way, smoke like snow

Tattooing their bodies with narcotic holiness,
The glaze of status, the faux lacquer of bliss.

I'm coming at you live frostbitten and thinking,
"Language is for losers." Who cannot think

Our elegies are endless endlessly and the words
We put to them too often unheard and hurried?

I'm coming at you live from the intangible.
Do you want to ride, or die crowded into a small

Space spitting, *Come with me*? One day my song
Will be called "Language Is for Lovers." One

Day desire will not be a form of wickedness.
And when you offer your drug, O Ghost, I'll resist.

THE LAST TRAIN TO AFRICA

after Elizabeth Alexander

doesn't leave the train station, according to the story
Stagger tells, until tomorrow morning. We shoot up 23
North, singing our version of Tribe, put pedal to floor
doing a buck fifty, Stagger's braids in a red bandanna,

chrome on the rims, the cab smoky, the volume rolled
to its end. Beyond the insomniac nuclear silos built against
nature where the wind tastes like roadkill or tiny bowls
of fire, a gun in the glove box, there is no one badder

than Stagger speeding across two counties until I can see
he's getting staggerly. I drive the rest of the way, pedal to floor,
because his train to Africa is leaving before she can please
him. We stop at a drive-through strip club where the poor and

lonely are working. Naked, jaded, sea-hag-looking sisters,
only one of them pretty, a dark chocolate chattering girl.
Stagger spends the next hour soaking his money in her
skin. Between there and Africa Simpson, all his questions

amount to, "What's someone like you doing here with the aunts
of poverty?" To which each of her answers sounds like "Rent."
I had no money, but the whole time I napped she was haunt-
ing my body. I was so fucked up then, even the reflections

of truckers were godlike to me. She was one of my nieces,
caught along a road named America or named Jemima,
bucking for bills or company with the rhythm of a rhesus
monkey. We made the train, but her image was still with me.

NEW FOLK

I said Folk was dressed in Blues but hairier and hemped.
After "We acoustic banjo disciples!" Jebediah said, "When
and whereforth shall the bucolic blacks with good tempers
come to see us pluck as Elizabeth Cotten intended?"
We stole my Uncle Windchime's minivan, penned a simple
ballad about the drag of lovelessness, and drove the end
of the Chitlin' Circuit to a joint skinny as a walk-in temple
where our new folk was not that new, but strengthened
by our twelve-bar conviction. A month later, in pulled
a parade of well-meaning alabaster post-adolescents.
We noticed the sand-tanned and braless ones piled
in the ladder-backed front row with their boyfriends
first because beneath our twangor slept what I'll call
a hunger for the outlawable. One night J asked me when
sisters like Chapman would arrive. I shook my chin wool
then, and placed my hand over the guitar string's wind-
ow till it stilled. "When the moon's black," I said. "Be faithful."

A PLATE OF BONES

My silk slick black muscular back-
talking uncle driving me and a school
of fish corpses to church. The sick-eyed
gap-mouthed bass, the kingfish without
kingdom, the sliver-thin silver fish—each
dead and separate in a cool bucket. Gilded
and shapely as a necktied Sunday morning,
the fish. *Sit upright*, he said, and I sat right up,
riding shotgun looking hard at the road.
He muttered, *Crackers,* as if it was something
swinging from a thin clear wire,
the clump of tiny maggots in a trout's brain,
the flies lazing like the devil's jewelry at our backs.

Last night when the white boy's arm
lassoed his daughter's neck, my uncle
said nothing until they left. I let him feed me
the anger I knew was a birthright,
a plate of bones thin enough to puncture
a lung. But the words did things in my mouth
I'd heard they killed people for. They went
to a movie and sat quietly and touched
or did not touch in the darkness. My uncle watched
the news with the sound turned down
until she came in, my silk slick black back-
talking cousin, his daughter. He went to work
beating a prayer out of her skin.

THE SHEPHERD

"I am here, in my father's house."

—"*The Sheep-Child,*" *by James Dickey*

If you and every person in the county mailed
me an envelope of five to ten dollars, I think
I could rehabilitate the sheep. You should know,
however, that they are mentioned over three hundred times
in the Bible. Remember when John the Baptist
sees Jesus coming toward him and says,
"Behold, the Lamb of God, who takes away the sin
of the world"? Lambs, which is to say sheep,
are mentioned twenty-eight times in the Book of Revelation
alone. I like the wily black sheep of the shepherd boy
who lacked training as well as the brooding sheep
at the insomniac's fence. Sheep strike
the same pose each season: sheared and suspended
from hooks like strange fruit or fidgeting in open fields
like boys in oversize baseball uniforms.
What if your momma tried to make you join a pony
league of ten- to twelve-year-olds who were coached
by a man they knew as "Coach" and you knew
as a wolf sweating your mother's body?
Whenever my parents fought, my father would drive me
to the dollar movies to watch and forget the movies.
The rain left stripes on our faces. The news
of another sheep's death was often on my mind.
The story of how sheep fall in love with moonlight;
how sheep go astray and are bruised.
My father sometimes burned upon the sofa
like a campfire, and a dry whimper
broke from him. Sometimes in mid conversation,
sheep begin drifting off to sleep. You say, "Sunshine,"

and their eyes roll over the horizon. I love the sheep
of the lost lake and the sheep of patron saints.
Once my mother bought a sheepskin brush
for my father's sheepskin jacket. He held her then,
as if she were a shepherd's guitar. My love is sentimental.
It is the good news that holds us. I am still in the house
with the music that makes my brown face soft
and gives the sheep a reason to believe. How, Mr. Dickey,
would you have told your father about your pet
imaginary sheep the day you kneeled in the backyard
with a choked hose and thirsty bucket, him saying,
"How 'bout playing football or basketball if not baseball?"
and you yielding to nothing, you shaking your wooly head
above the emptiness, half hearing the wind mutter, "Punk,"
or your father mutter it, and when the water came finally,
you crying, your father walking out of the fence?

HIDE

The tire was like the wet hide of a seal

dropped from the bridge

to waters as black as a seal

glistening that way in the wake

of sparkling nighttime dead

if a thing can be that dead

in the same breath the limp tire

damned and dropped from the rail

the night we ran away rolled

from the three-wheeled scampering Ford

like a gawking with no face

like a hole to the place you wanted to live

I was the wet hide too in a seal

of shadows on broad river bridge

sleepy as the drowned and black

listening that way to the wakefulness

dead if wakefulness can be that dead

and lit the nighttime littered with breaking

and tired of running away of being rolled

from a damp dream by fists and scampering

to my gawking shoes as you led me

from our house with a flat line across your face

the heart weary of its grief desires forgetfulness

but I never wanted it to be that way

FOR BROTHERS OF THE DRAGON

a pecha kucha

[PREMONITION]
I dreamed my brother said I'd live with the feeling
a child feels the first time he sees his brother disappear.
I went down on my knees and sure enough, I was the size
of a boy again. With my shins like two skinny tracks in the dirt,
I could almost hear a train carrying its racket up my spine.

[OPENING SCENE]
The day Malcolm X was buried, his brothers were in a motel
watching the funeral on a black-and-white TV. If I were in their story,
I would have run down the assassins and removed their eyes.
It does not matter if this is true, only that it can be conceived.

[HOW FICTION FUNCTIONS]
However else fiction functions, it fills you with the sound
of crows chirping, *alive alive alive.* But that's temporary too.
Tell my story, begs the past, as if it was a prayer
for an imagined life or a life that's better than the life you live.

[SCENE AT THE GRAVE]
I am considering writing a story about the lives the brothers lead
afterward. They will change their names a third time and abandon
their families. They will visit their brother's grave at Ferncliff.
They will be poor and empty. One will bag the dead man's bones
while the one holding the shovel begs him to hurry.

[FORESHADOWING]
I keep thinking I'll have a dream about the smoke clouding
the bar my brother and I used to haunt. We spent hours saying
nothing. He pretended he didn't know the man raising us was

his father but not mine. Instead I dream about the mouth
of a dragon, the smoke of a train vanishing into a mountainside.

[DRAMATIC ARC]
One brother will want, at first, redemption; one brother will want,
at first, revenge. Their story will be part family saga and elegy,
part mystery. What changes them before the story begins will be,
at first, more important than what changes them when it ends.

[IMAGERY]
I have no problem with the flaws of memory. The bird carcass
stiff as the shoe of a hit-and-run victim on the side of the road
might just be a veil the wind pulled from the face of a new bride.
Why was the imagination invented, if not to remake?

[OPENING DIALOGUE]
The motel's twin beds will be narrow and dingy. On each pillow
will be a sweating peppermint candy left by a desk clerk
who will sigh the way my mother sighs. "Y'all look like the ghosts
of Malcolm X," I'll have her think, carelessly. "Y'all smell
like men who slept all night in a boxcar or on a roadside."

[SYMBOLISM]
However else fiction functions, it fills you with the sound
of running away. The dirt, the smudged mirror, even the silences
between speech have something to say. In novels
there is no such thing as a useless past or typical day.

[FLASHBACK]
I'm thinking of black boys in the countryside with a white boy
who'd seen, only a summer before, a black man strung up
at the edge of town. They'll be singing when they drag the white boy
to the river and throw him in. They'll be singing when they
dive in and drag him back to shore before he drowns.

[STATIC CHARACTERS]

In my novel all the minor characters will look like various friends
and family: Blind Vince Twang, BlackerThanMost, Deadeye Sue,
Lil Clementine. They will be more human than my protagonists
because they will be left with lives that do not change.

[POINT OF VIEW]

The chin of Malcolm's widow will quiver below her veil.
Where is home now? she'll think. It will be the wind
or her trembling that moves the veil. I am not going to describe
her face because I want you to think of her as a bride.

[SETTING THAT ILLUMINATES CHARACTER]

When I try remembering dirt, I remember my mother's pale carpet
stained by mud and my brother on his knees with a hairbrush
and bar of soap, scrubbing before school. I do not remember
the names of the birds who lived outside our house,
but I know their music was swallowed by the passing trains.

[ALLEGORY]

One brother will tell the other a story: *Once, in the shadow of a tree
lit with song, when a black woman unbuttoned her blouse,
all the birds came to dine.* It will mean there are people who root
and people who roam; people bound to a place
and people bound to an idea, whatever the idea may be.

[CONNOTATION]

I wish I was not the kind of man who abandons
those who love him repeatedly. My brother must be
one hundred pounds heavier now than he was
all those years ago. Because growing old is like slipping
into a new coat without taking the old coat off,
I think of him bearing the weight of our family.

[DELETED CHAPTER]

You'll find salt in the eyes of anyone who kneels too long
with his head in the dirt. I should say what happened
to my brother when he was sixteen. My mother found him
naked and weeping to himself in the closet. Because
I wasn't there, there is no suitable place in the story for this scene.

[FALLING ACTION]

Later both X brothers show up at the widow X's door and miss
the softer woman she was before. Here, I am not going to say
she forgives them. When she turns them away, I imagine
the sunlight bleeding its heaviness upon their backs.

[METAPHOR]

Because I am a brother of the dragon, call me Dragonfly.
When I dream of the train riding our parallel spines, carrying
our history, the weight that turns my brother into fire, makes me
scattered light. In my story the X brothers will live
without their brother, but that doesn't mean they'll survive.

[ALLUSION TO THEME]

It's all true: the pair of tracks through the darkness,
men who look like me, disguised. The bewilderment
that cannot be described. What I feel is *Why*. In fiction
everything happens with ease, and the easefulness kills me.

[RESOLUTION]

I am full of dirt sometimes. I am trying to tell you a story
without talking. I promise nothing I write about you
tomorrow will be a lie. Instead of fiction, brother,
I will offer you an apology. And if that fails,
I will drag myself to your arms crying, *Speak to me*.

THREE MEASURES OF TIME

I. How My Brother Tells Time

By noon and the hours jumping toward dinner bells.
By the goodness in the body smelling sweet
as the air around our mother's good-night sentence,

the one long since gone flat as money,
the belly shrouded in hunger.

The past is nutritious; the past is there on the table
with the hair you know is Ma's color.
It's curling and somewhere she is marveling

her light-headed, near comic hairdo.
Absence in each Hello, her teeth are yellow,

her belly stretch-marked, her glasses
were supposed to be scratch-proof and unbreakable.
She is in the kitchen cooking something

and singing, each pink note ringing through the rooms,
but it's not the kind of shoo-bee-doo-bees the radio loves

to spit at you. If she wrote the words down,
they'd be illegible, darkening, prideful. You might ask her
later if she'd finished dinner, but she'd already be asleep.

Let's wait in the hall outside her door with our plates.
No such thing as thanklessness. Let's sing until she's sound

awake, half brother. I am or I am almost the same as you.
The hour is hushed and clicking to rust
and cleaving and cleaving to her: the meat that made us.

II. How My Father Tells Time

By knowing how the year jumps forward.
God in the meat of a chicken. The smell

of barbecue in a sentence, the scent
long gone flat as money. Animal hunger
in the mouth like the hollow side of a bell.

And remorsefulness bland as the grease
on the carcass. The past has its nutrients,

but it is too thin for color, and it is shapeless.
Like wind troubling my mother's hairdo
when she looks at you sideways,

a gathering storm in each Hello.
The day is yellow, but it is not scratch-proof

or unbreakable. By the time the coals die down
you're asleep before a whispering TV.
No such thing as darkening.

Let's sing the old songs until the hour is new.
Step-Daddy, half of me belongs to you.

III. How My Mother Tells Time

By none of the hours jumping at the window.

By the joblessness of God and the body
beneath a floral bedsheet. A sentence

with no sense of anything but money.
A mouth of bad teeth and a past bland
as grease in hair too thin for color.

Sleep is a form of absence.
Nothing sings without food.

You are in the kitchen with a spatula
above something inedible or inevitable
and darkening. Or you are asleep

in a locked room. O Blood,
the hours cling to you.

[GOD IS AN AMERICAN]

THE AVOCADO

"In 1971, drunk on the sweet, sweet juice of revolution,
a crew of us marched into the president's office with a list
of demands," the black man tells us at the February luncheon,
and I'm pretending I haven't heard this one before as I eye
black tortillas on a red plate beside a big green bowl
of guacamole made from the whipped, battered remains
of several harmless former avocados. If abolitionists had a flag
it would no doubt feature the avocado, also known as the alligator
pear, for obvious reasons. "Number one: reparations!
Enough gold to fill each of our women's wombs, gold
to nurse our warriors waiting to enter this world with bright fists,
that's what we told them," the man says, and I'm thinking
of the money-colored flesh of the avocado, high in monosaturates;
its oil content is second only to olives. I am looking
at Yoyo's caterpillar locks dangle over her ear. I dare you
to find a lovelier black woman from Cincinnati, where the North
touches the South. "Three: we wanted more boulevards
named for the Reverend Dr. Martin Luther King Jr. An airport
named for Sojourner Truth." The roots of the avocado tree
can raise pavement, so it's not too crazy to imagine the fruit
as a symbol of revolt on the abolitionist flag. We are all one kind
of abolitionist or another, no doubt. And we are like the avocado too
with its inedible ruby-colored seed that can actually sprout from inside
when the fruit is overmature, causing internal molds and breakdown.
"Demand number twenty-one: a Harriet Tubman statue on the mall!"
Brother man is weeping now and walking wet tissue to the trash can
and saying, "Harriet Tubman was a walking shadow," or, "Harriet Tubman
walked in shadows," or, "To many, Harriet Tubman was a shadow
to walk in," and the meaning is pureed flesh with lime juice,
minced garlic, and chili powder; it is salt, and the pepper
Harriet Tubman tossed over her shoulder to trouble the bloodhounds.

Many isolated avocado trees fail to fruit from lack of pollination.
"Goddamn, ain't you hungry?" I whisper to Yoyo, and she puts a finger
to my lips to distract me. Say, baby, wasn't that you waking me up
last night to say you'd had a dream where I was a big luscious man-
size avocado? Someone's belly is growling. "We weren't going
to be colored, we weren't going to be Negro," the man says,
and I'm thinking every time I hear this story it's the one telling the story
that's the hero. "Hush now," Harriet Tubman probably said
near dawn, pointing a finger black enough to be her pistol barrel
toward the future or pointing a pistol barrel black enough
to be her finger at the mouth of some starved, stammering slave
and then lifting her head to listen for something no one but her could hear.

A HOUSE IS NOT A HOME

It was the night I embraced Ron's wife a bit too long
because he'd refused to kiss me good-bye
that I realized the essential nature of sound.
When she slapped me across one ear
and he punched me in the other, I recalled,
almost instantly, the purr of liquor sliding
along the neck of the bottle a few hours earlier
as the three of us took turns imitating the croon
of the recently deceased Luther Vandross.
I decided then, even as my ears fattened,
to seek employment at the African-American
Acoustic and Audiological Accident Insurance Institute,
where probably there is a whole file devoted
to Luther Vandross. And probably it contains
the phone call he made once to ask a niece
the whereabouts of his very first piano.
I already know there is a difference
between hearing and listening,
but to get the job, I bet I will have to learn
how to transcribe church fires or how to categorize
the dozen or so variations of gasping, one of which
likely includes Ron and me in the eighth grade—
the time a neighbor flashed her breasts at us.
That night at Ron's house I believed he, his wife,
and Luther loved me more than anything
I could grasp. "I can't believe you won't kiss me;
you're the gayest man I know!" I told him,
just before shackling my arms around his wife.
"My job is all about context," I will tell friends
when they ask. "I love it, though most days
all I do is root through noise like a termite

with a number on his back." What will I steal?
Rain falling on a picket sign, breathy epithets—
you think I'm bullshitting. When you have no music,
everything becomes a form of music. I bet
somewhere in Mississippi there is a skull
that only a sharecropper's daughter can make sing.
I'll steal that sound. More than anything,
I want to work at the African-American
Acoustic and Audiological Accident Insurance Institute
so that I can record the rumors and raucous rhythms
of my people, our jangled history, the slander
in our sugar, the ardor in our anger, a subcategory
of which probably includes the sound particular to one
returning to his feet after a friend has knocked him down.

CARP POEM

After I have parked below the spray paint caked in the granite
grooves of the Frederick Douglass Middle School sign,

where men-size children loiter like shadows draped in outsize
denim, jerseys, braids, and boots that mean I am no longer young;

after I have made my way to the New Orleans Parish Jail down the block,
where the black prison guard wearing the same weariness

my prison guard father wears buzzes me in, I follow his pistol and shield
along each corridor trying not to look at the black men

boxed and bunked around me until I reach the tiny classroom
where two dozen black boys are dressed in jumpsuits orange as the carp

I saw in a pond once in Japan, so many fat, snaggletoothed fish
ganged in and lurching for food that a lightweight tourist could have crossed

the water on their backs so long as he had tiny rice balls or bread
to drop into the mouths below his footsteps, which I'm thinking

is how Jesus must have walked on the lake that day, the crackers and crumbs
falling from the folds of his robe, and how maybe it was the one fish

so hungry it leaped up his sleeve that he later miraculously changed
into a narrow loaf of bread, something that could stick to a believer's ribs,

and don't get me wrong, I'm a believer too, in the power of food at least,
having seen a footbridge of carp packed gill to gill, packed tighter

than a room of boy prisoners waiting to talk poetry with a young black poet, packed so close they'd have eaten each other had there been nothing else to eat.

THE ELEGANT TONGUE

It's Yoyo who says Tonguing, a form of kissing
favored among the half-lit young, is mostly overrated
and rarely practiced among married folk like us,
but we give it a try, clumsy as two elephants swapping
gin-tinged saliva Friday night to prove the idea
is always better than the act, and since I am wistful
as the blind old lumberjack who touched the elephant's knee
and fumbling for his ax declared, *This animal is most like a tree*,
I remember my tongue sandpapered against vowels in a mouth
named Yolanda in the dark of a yellow bus long ago,
and I tell Yoyo how that girl may still be somewhere thinking fondly
of our tangle. Forgive me: I believe, as the elephant must,
that everything is punctured by the tusks of Nostalgia.
They use those things to uproot roots, but let's never forget
the old blind warrior who touched the elephant's tusk
and said, *This thing is most like a spear,* and took it as a sign
that Man should spend his life defending his house,
and though he probably wasn't wrong, it's the best intentions
that turn need into want, which is another way of saying
the tongue is mostly disgust coated in desire,
or desire coated in disgust depending on the way you look.
My tongue is unusually short, but I'm happy to say
Yoyo prefers my lips. If you are not an elephant more adept
at using your trunk than your tongue, you cannot wrestle,
nor caress, nor blow water into the air while your kiss
is being chewed in a dining room beside a houseplant
called *The Mother-in-Law's Tongue* because of its sword-shaped
leaves or perhaps because it has no mind for boundaries,
though boundaries too are a matter of the way you look.
The African elephant, for example, can be found in countries
like Angola, Botswana, Cameroon, Ethiopia, Ghana, Kenya,

Mali, Nigeria, Rwanda, Senegal, Somalia, South Africa,
and Zimbabwe, and that must mean a tongue knows
nothing about territory. It's a spit of land, a promontory.
Remember the blind prisoner who touched the elephant's flank
and said, *This creature is most like a wall,* and believed it
meant all the world must be a jail? Some say it's mostly walls
that constitute a marriage, and in many ways that may be true,
since Yoyo will not divulge the slip and slither administered once
by a boy plucked from the pews of her serious Pentecostal history,
which I know featured a perspiring, eye-tossing glossolalist
mouthing things only the faithful could decipher so that *Fuck*
might be translated as the sound at the beginning
of *Forgiveness,* and the hands of the white-bloused ladies,
her momma among them, patting the convulser's shoulders,
might be said to emulate several vibrating reeds.
I'm talking about the rapture of tongues. The Holy Rollers
say it's most like a flame in the devil's blackout
because in Acts, tongues of fire are said to alight on the apostles,
filling them with the Holy Spirit and allowing them to speak
in a language understood by foreigners from several countries.
Darling, kiss me again in the nastiest possible way.
When the blind fondle the elephant's trunk, an organ
of fifteen thousand miraculous multipurpose muscles, and hiss,
This creature is most like the serpent in Eden,
tell them, *If there is goodness in your heart, it will come
to your mouth,* and if that doesn't work, tell them,
In the dark it's not the forked tongue that does the piercing.

MYSTIC BOUNCE

Even if you love the racket of ascension,
you must know how the power leaves you.
And at this pitch, who has time for meditation?
The sea walled in by buildings. I do miss
the quiet. Don't you? When I said, "Fuck the deer
antlered and hithered in fur," it was because
I had seen the faces of presidents balled into a fist.
If I were in charge, I would know how to fix
the world: free health care or free physicals,
at least, and an abiding love for the abstract.
When I said, "All of history is saved for us,"
it was because I scorned the emancipated sky.
Does the anthem choke you up? When I asked
God if anyone born to slaves would die
a slave, He said, "Sure as a rock descending
a hillside." That's why I'm not a Christian.

ANCHOR HEAD

Because keyless and clueless,
because trampled in gunpowder
and hoof-printed address,

from Australopithecus or Adam's
dim boogaloo to birdsong
and what the bird boogaloos to,

because I was waiting to break
these legs free, one to each
shore, to be head-dressed in sweat,

my work, a form of rhythm
like the first sex, like the damage
of death and distance

and depression, of troubled
instances and blind instruction,
of pleasure and placelessness,

because I was off-key and careless
and learning through leaning,
because I was astral and pitchforked

and packaged to a dim bungalow
of burden and if not burden,
the dim boredom of no song,

I became a salt-worn dream-
anchor, I leaped overboard
in my shackles and sailed

through my reflection on down
to ruin, calling out to God,
and then calling out no more.

A FORM OF SEXUAL HEALING

for Marvin Gaye

Will you speak to me now bedeviling, sweet muser?
Old coke-face up in the song bar all karaoked in discord,
Your music lavished by a boozehound whose singing

Is syncless, whose outcry eradicates your ghost-
Written dabblings. The difference between

"What's Going On" and "Let's Get It On" is filled
With semen and a chorus of maidens in makeup chanting,
WakeupWakeupWakeup. Like an echo disrobed, like a man

On his back and a woman breaking against his pose—
Tonight when I heard you, whose singing was hunger,

I cried for more than a moment over the forms of healing
Because my crush was demised, because my joy was capsized,
And the feeling made me clean as your voice on its side.

Will you speak to me now, soul-musing bedeviler,
From that hole out of which all the prisons of the world arise?

TWENTY MEASURES OF CHITCHAT

a pecha kucha

[THE MAGIC OF MAGIC]

When everything is a spell, when my cries reverse
in mid cry (and here I am talking voodoo),
I wake as a small black dog shucked in uncertainty,
feverish, grown sick of monotony and words like *time*.

[SQUAT]

You may think back when there were twenty tribes
in twenty square miles of land speaking twenty
different languages, life was all that, but you'd be wrong.
Everyone was thinking, "What do they think of me?"

[MORNING ALARM]

When everything dope as a trifle of fangs
is disrupted by bells and the blinging
which is the other side of a dream,
I am beside myself with the daze the day begets.

[THEY'RE ON THEIR WAY THERE]

When the day is spooked and hooded in cloud (a hot mess),
the dream's patchwork dispatched, the felt of a feeling,
when it's possible each of us is a protagonist, in what
ways will our *whats* differ from one another?

[EVERYTHING HAPPENS TO ME]

In the portable book I read how blacks were troubled
by none of the troubles of today. To become invisible, it said,
one need only walk through rain. I tried this, but it did not work.
I chased the dream, but when I woke, the spell endured.

[LUNCHING]

I was scratching our name into the bark of a tree.
I was throwing up and down on my hands and knees like a soul
who is not a ghost yet. I wouldn't have made it without those
tiny tablets. I swallowed four, and then, baby, I was good to go.

[RULES FOR SUCCESS]

"Have you ever done a thing so much you learn to do it
without thinking?" you ask. And then: "What do you know
about inaction in action?" But what I hear is:
"If at first you don't succeed, keep on sucking till you do."

[QUESTIONS FOR FURTHER STUDY]

I heard you ask, "Why was the dream invented,
if not to undo?" My mouth opened like the hole
in the wall you were punching. I barked at the shadows,
a foot fell above us, the ghosts came back.

[LANDSCAPE WITH RIOT]

When the house windows were broken, I was one of the people
stepping in, then out again, with boxes and whole registers
of what belonged to me, with dream-swollen jewelry leashed
about my neck, with blood on my shirt and blood on my teeth.

[THE IMMINENT TILL]

Time is the real cannibal, mesmerizing even at face value,
weighing down the stars, and the river holding the unlucky
body attached to a cluster of fish, where the heart is
so diluted the doctors wear gloves when they handle it.

[ANTIGRAVITY MACHINE]

When I float like a lost balloon looking to become invisible
(default sleep, default air, default black), it is the hour
there's enough darkness to click the headlights on,
and enough light you cannot see the light they make yet.

[GHOST HARDWARE]

"Given a soul for, at the start, nothing, it will be all uphill
heaving vapor," you say. "Daylight caked in the whip
and eyelashes, the voice of somebodiness wired deep
in the bones, a breath that makes everything green."

[SEEDS IN A RAINSTICK]

When I pant, "What now?" with my big ear to the door
of your body as in a cup filled with listening (pregnable),
and the tremble rides my whiskied vowel, what your body is
runs down my thickness ruinously and sweetly.

[A MONTH OF SUNDAYS]

Including the low hollow of sighing (singing) figures
figuring (hollering) moving forward while moving backward
for a god who demands a constant and singular praise,
all the head holds, and all the lyrics of rejoicing.

[LAMENTO]

When my wind-scuffed wig mingles in halfhearted tufts
with the dust (the shock of growing old without growing);
when the shine is greased in the aesthetics of whatever
grief calls itself (grief), I know the sublime is approaching.

[A HISTORY OF SELF-RELIANCE]

The façade of solitude: a serious black man
reading a book at happy hour in a bar. The façade
of newness: pier stilts along the Mississippi painted
so white, you have to touch them to know their age.

[WESTERN WIND]

Since it is true that waiting on the dead requires living,
true that death means in its way, we are alive or will grasp,
when the future arrives, what it means to be dead,
call me to your arms, and I will come fiercely sweetly.

[EVENING ALARM]

We tumble across the mattress unfazed. You treat me
like a fix. We set to licking. We nix the ticktock. Your socks
rolled down to your toes, I love your nose. We steal fire
and walk until the path levitates. Our feet light up the place.

[VIOLETS FOR YOUR VIOLETS]

When what your body is flowers in its garment of scent,
when your hot polka-dot dime-store dress fills
with duskiness like the idea of a net (cape), I want to drag
my bone across your path (and here I'm telling you the truth).

[THE SHAPE OF THE HEAD]

When I said my past was a severed tail, I had my eyes
closed, so the lie wouldn't sting. When I had my head
between your knees, I was looking for where it was
I'd come from, and how it was I could escape.

NOTHING

which is what the first idiot says
to the second idiot in the joke
I have made up but will not share

with you when the scent of another
of those full-boned marital truths
hovers in the air between us.

I feel the joke knock around and expand
in my gut, pushing all the good air out.
I'd rather be a blind girl, Etta James sings

somewhere, and no one is willing
to eat or dance because almost everyone is
sleeping: my single-breasted mother

in her soft blue shirt, my stepfather
in his soft shoe blues a floor below her.
I love the way a good song makes you

say nothing. And I believe happiness
is not the same thing as success.
I feel the joke walk in ahead of us

when we enter your parents' house,
where the big bed fills the bedroom
and the big TV fills the den

and the Sundays are filled with *Amen*.
Sometimes when we are sitting
with our heads bowed over dinner

I can hear nothing: not God
saying you are blessed,
not the meat cooling, not your parents'

nor our own breathing. I love the way love
makes us say nothing like a good song,
but I believe it could be fear. Some nights

I lie on my belly in the darkness of our room,
my cheek to the pillow, my head to the wall,
you waiting, and me saying it to you.

GOD IS AN AMERICAN

I still love words. When we make love in the morning,
your skin damp from a shower, the day calms.
Schadenfreude may be the best way to name the covering
of adulthood, the powdered sugar on a black shirt. I am

alone now on the top floor pulled by obsession, the ink
on my fingers. Sometimes what I feel has a difficult name.
Sometimes it is like the world before America, the kin-
ship of God's fools and guardians, of hooligans; the dreams

of mothers with no children. A word can be the boot print
in a square of fresh cement and the glaze of morning.
Your response to my kiss is, *I have a cavity.* I am in
love with incompletion. I am clinging to your moorings.

Yes, I have a pretty good idea what beauty is. It survives
all right. It aches like an open book. It makes it difficult to live.

[COFFIN FOR HEAD OF STATE]

LIGHTHEAD'S GUIDE TO ADDICTION

And if you are addicted to sleep, a bay of fresh coffee may help.
If you are addicted to coffee, teach yourself to breakdance.
If you are addicted to dancing, polio will cure you.
If you hear that the last black man alive will be burned at sunset,
find an underground railroad.
If you are addicted to railroads, try wearing undersized shoes.
No one knows where your mother has gone with her tax refund.
If you are addicted to shoes, move to a provincial village in Japan.
If you are addicted to Japan, try eating with no teeth.
If you are addicted to teeth, visit the wife beater's widow;
she will be upstairs awaiting your caress.
I often wake up horny. If you are addicted to masturbation, seek company.
If you are addicted to company, try starlight and silence.
If you are addicted to silence, find guard dogs, traffic, or infants.
If you are addicted to infants, try reliable contraception.
Or try asking yourself: *What's wrong with me?*
If you are addicted to contraception, try recklessness.
Try riding an unsaddled horse until you are thrown into a bed of gravel.
If you are addicted to recklessness, try a spoon-fed disease.
My mother loves imagining the day she'll die.
If you are addicted to disease, visit an Old World doctor.
If you are addicted to doctors, try war.
If you are addicted to sorrow, all my talk about loss is not loss to you.
No one knows why your father built a shed for his weapons.
Probably was some hellified form of addiction.
If you are addicted to weapons, please find the people who plan to burn
the last black man alive at sunset for me.
Or try learning a little history.
Obviously, I'm addicted to repetition. Which is a form for history.
If you are addicted to history, try a blindfold of razors or buy a Cadillac.
If you are addicted to Cadillacs, try poverty.

No one is addicted to poverty, but if you are, try wealth.

If you are addicted to wealth, you'll need money.

If you are addicted to money, you'll need money. Try that.

LINER NOTES FOR AN IMAGINARY PLAYLIST

for R

1. "Wind Solo" by The Felonious Monks
      From the album *Silense* © 1956
1945, after everyone got hip to the blues, this is the code
The hipsters devised. This is what they call a mean
Horn. High on something, the sax man wades beyond the shallow
End of a stormy sea. You can almost see him gathering mist.
The album cover's got nothing but the contours of his body
And a dangerous language you comprehend even if you can't read.

2. "The DJ's PJs" by SGP (the Stank Gangsta Prankstas)
      From the album *Loot the Joker* © 1992
This is for shell-toe sneakers and warm-ups dyed the hottest red
I ever saw. So red it was cool. So cool it was a permanent cold.
You can almost hear Negroes freed of the ghetto, the mint
Spewing greenbacks in this song. Who wouldn't want to shampoo
In Benjamins? Even one hit and a dope video makes a mystic
Of the pauper. When it's over, you can hear someone tipping a bottle.

3. "Mood Etude #5" by Fred Washington Sr.
      From the album *Blassics* © 1985
Strange inclusion, I know, but sometimes lyrics wear a blindfold.
How many violins, harps, and grand pianos constitute a jazz reed?
This is Bach according to a young man born on the Carolina coast.
This is Bach according to a man whose favorite word is *Amen.*
This is Bach according to a man whose childhood was a shambles.
What if Keats heard jazz? What if Bach heard the blues? It's all music.

4. "Metal Face" by Glad Battle Wounds
      From the album *New Battle* © 2004
Remember the Mute Trout album *Empty (MT)*? The mystique

Of this jam won't puzzle you if you do. The way the battle
For hearts and minds sounds like the same old bullshit. A newsreel
Of tanks crushing corpses and a brave soldier in a coat
Of medals. Remember those old war songs about the Age of Man?
Maybe like those cuts this one is about being bold and shackled.

5. "Oh, You" by Marvin & the Gay Ghosts
        From the album *Baby, Don't Won't* © 1987
Everything that needs to be said here is contained in a shadow.
Whenever I fell asleep listening to this song, I woke drenched in music,
The CD on repeat, my mouth filled with the meat of the bitter-
Sweet. I'd dream of my first love, then find none of it was real.
Some songs are like that, I suppose. Like being clothed
In sweat and wistfulness. Sigh. It's a tune to make you moan.

6. "Mythic Blues" by Big Bruise Guitar
        From the album *The Devil's Angel* © 1924
If you're happy, skip this one. It's definitely not meant
To make you dance. Yes, the previous track was also slow. Use the shuffle
Mode if you don't want to walk the path I've left you. Called "Mythic
Blues," this track has a way of reminding you how sin does battle
With the good in you. Saltwater is all a listener can reap.
You can see nothing but the blues even when your eyes are closed.

Friend, sometimes the wind's scuttle makes the reeds
In the body vibrate. Sometimes the noise gives up its code
And the music is better at saying what I mean to say.

SATCHMO RETURNS TO NEW ORLEANS

You are the greasy Daddy of Jazz, Peasy Daddy.
You are the brassy Mother of Jazz, the bellowing bastard of jazz,

Sweet-trumpeting strumpet of jazz, Easy Daddy;
A hankie full of toots and zooting, Mister Sadmo;

And I shall never blame America for not loving and then loving you;
Nor shall I blame the Mississippi, nor the dens of Chicago,

Nor your eight-mile storyville grin, nor your Zulu blackface,
Mister Black Face. I shall not blame the "Cake Walk Blues"

Nor the "Saint Louis Blues," St. Louis. I shall not blame
The "Moonlight Blues," nor the "Starlight Blues," nor the "Midnight Blues,"

Nor "Mack the Knife," nor the switchblade in your pocket,
Nor the pale moon shining on the fields below,

Mr. Press-Me-to-Your-Heart Sweet-Louisiana: I've got no reason
To be blue. Nor shall I blame the heebie-jeebies

Of the West Coast Negro, nor shall I blame the wide eye
Of the banjo, nor shall I blame the band's spit-shined

"When the Saints Go Marching In," played as if it wasn't at first
A funeral song, and finished somewhere near closing time

With "La Vie en Rose," your heart so broken again
You doze on the cab ride home and dream the notes

To "West End Blues," which is what an American city sounds like
At 45 mph after dark when your eyes are closed.

FISH HEAD FOR KATRINA

The mouth is where the dead
Who are not dead do not dream

A house of damaged translations
Task married to distraction

As in a bucket left in a storm
A choir singing in the rain like fish

Acquiring air under water
Prayer and sin the body

Performs to know it is alive
Lit from the inside by reckoning

As in a city
Which is no longer a city

The tongue reaching down a tunnel
And the teeth wet as windows

Set along a highway
Where the dead live in the noise

Of their shotgun houses
They drift from their wards

Like fish spreading thin as a song
Diminished by its own opening

Split by faith and soaked in it
The mouth is a flooded machine

SNOW FOR WALLACE STEVENS

No one living a snowed-in life
can sleep without a blindfold.
Light is the lion that comes down to drink.
I know *tink and tank and tunk-a-tunk-tunk*
holds nearly the same sound as a bottle.
Drink and drank and drunk-a-drunk-drunk,
light is the lion that comes down.
This song is for *the wise man who avenges*
by building his city in snow.
For his decorations in a nigger cemetery.
How, with pipes of winter
lining his cognition, does someone learn
to bring a sentence to its knees?
Who is not more than his limitations?
Who is not the blood in a wine barrel
and the wine as well? I too, having lost faith
in language, have placed my faith in language.
Thus, I have a capacity for love without
forgiveness. This song is for my foe,
the clean-shaven, gray-suited, gray patron
of Hartford, the emperor of whiteness
blue as a body made of snow.

TANKHEAD

As General Patton you will be expected to give
his D-day speech to park audiences twice a day.
To fit in the costume you will have to eat nothing
but haggis, a Scottish dish consisting of the minced heart,
lungs, and liver of a sheep.

It may be that visitors love our General Patton best
because of the huge, mightily polished helmet bobbing on a head
twice the size of the body. Notice the cut of his riding pants,
the angle of his cavalry boots. Boys love the nickle-plated Colt
and the .357 Magnum our Old Blood and Guts pretends to fire.
Fathers love the shimmer of his two dozen medals.

The general's swagger will become second nature to you.
Carrying such an enormous head, your body will seem
drunk on patriotism. Which is appropriate, since Patton walked funny.
He walked like a man who dislikes humor aimed at himself.
He was very self-conscious and believed his high-pitched voice
made soldiers think of their grandmothers.
Patton was not a singer because of his teeth.

"We can no more understand a Russian than a Chinese
or a Japanese, and from what I have seen of them,
I have no particular desire to understand them
except to ascertain how much lead or iron it takes to kill them,"
Patton liked to say. People of all creeds are welcomed here,
of course. You would be shocked to know
that our best Patton performer ever was a thin Asian girl.

Herodotus, who loved tales of battle, foresaw Patton's death
in a dream: the 2½-ton truck mashing his Cadillac outside Mannheim

in 1945, the clouds' warble, Old Blood and Guts
paralyzed from the neck down and covered in rain.
I have seen his big head left like a broken sarcophagus
outside the break room by spineless performers.

Herodotus noted that early sarcophagi
were carved from a special kind of rock
that consumed the flesh of the corpse inside.
This should give you a sense of what it will mean
to spend your days in the head of Patton.

His favorite animal was the armadillo.
He called Robert E. Lee Jesus. He fell in love
with Dwight Eisenhower between 1935 and 1940.
Distrustful of civilians, Patton measured everything
according to the shaft of his weapon. His word for penis was tank.
His motto was "Lead me, follow me, or get out of my way."

TWENTY-SIX IMAGINARY T-SHIRTS

1) Anonymous 2) Written in blue ballpoint
on a Band-Aid: DOWN WITH GRAVITY!
3) Breathing Expert for Hire 4) Profile of a man
with a Chihuahua hanging from his chin
5) Don't Misbehave Tonight 6) Die and Learn
7) The best way to wipe out poverty is to
wipe out poor people. Signed—the GOP 8) MUST SEE:
Fully equipped fashionable sonnet with
gorgeous slant rhyme and modest allusions. Missing
half of last couplet. 9) I am no food. 10) I'm not shy,
I'm sober. 11) A face half Ali circa *Rumble in the
Jungle,* half Elvis circa sequined Las Vegas
karate getup. Caption: *Float like a blue suede shoe.*
12) Let's pretend I'm still in love with youth.
13) IMMACULATE MATH: If Mary wakes an hour
early for a month, at the end of that month
Mary will have more than a day. How much time will
Mary have by May? 14) "This Is Not an Exit"
means "Do Not Enter." 15) A worm slinking from the left
nostril to the right above the caption: *May Enkidu find
no peace tonight.* 16) My hand wasn't in my ass, I was pulling
out my wallet! 17) Empty Pillbox. Caption: *FDA-approved
pill for inducing amnesia.* 18) The president in a blindfold
of lizards. Caption: QUANDARY 19) Freud's Auto
Repair Shop 20) Albert Einstein in snake-red
stilettos and lab coat above the caption: *Relatively
too much time.* 21) U.S. map above the caption:
*The only thing that fucks you
up more than poverty is wealth.* 22) Did you call me,
Valentine? 23) We won't get caught.

24) X for only one-third the pornography sold here.

25) You can have my husband, but please
don't mess with my man. 26) Zero preservatives.

MUSIC TO INTERROGATE BY

*When they ask what you did when you found the man
crouched at your door, his blood greening the steps,
you will have to say, He was not there; I did not see him.
The noise spread to the edge of the state. You had no —
power, but what you had was the same color as power,
like rain in the thread of a jacket. What did you do after
spitting out the name of your leader? Were there no
bullets to trouble him? Was there no spell to blind him?
When they ask what you did when you heard of the prisoners,
when you heard of the war against ideas, when they beat
strangers from their houses, what will you say? Who cares
about the fires beyond your porch? When the war spread
the brothers and fathers, blood of your age, to the borders,
what did you do? the children will ask. When the wafer
of destruction lay in your mouth, and the men in charge
charged men and sent men charging, when the field
was charged, the oil at its heart, the burials cocooned,
where were your feet? they'll ask, and what will you say?*

I will have to admit I was one of them. I believed the holes
would be erased. Our leader knew this floating up a mountain
on the backs of soldiers. I wanted only to be free, a cup of water,
if not rain. But the war spread to the edges of the state, narrow
closets opened in the field, the petals were white as cuffs.
What I had was the same as power, a dampness in the thread
of an old jacket. There was something sad and unforgiving
about our leader's accent, his short yellow tongue like a pencil
with no eraser. When they ask or wonder without asking
what I did when I saw the slick and shameful, the naked men
hanging an inch from the ground, when they ask what I did

when I heard of the prisoners, when I heard of the wars against
ideas, when they exiled strangers, what will I say? That's why
God et cetera? Who said you need not arm your children,
nor send them off to war? Who cares about the past worn
smooth by error and friction? The wafer of damage lay charged
in my mouth, bleeding its oil. I walked the back roads
of my property with one shoe untied and the other in my hand.

THE MUSTACHE

Nightshade sash, velvet patch
In the complexion. You might feel
Yourself vanish into the diesel fog,

The obliterating light and dark of it.
Shadow carved by what divides
The mind and tongue. As if suspended

Less than an inch above the speech,
As if the lip could bear so much history.
For instance, black as the smartest

Girl in class. Black as Hitler's cowlick
Or black as the valance falling from a widow's
Window. Black as the house sacked

Behind that window, and the boots
Coming and going on the stairs,
Or the breathing of a boy locked

In the mirror. Someone washing
His hands wearing black gloves.
The smell of greased metal, smoke

So thick it thins but does not vanish,
Black as a train snaking beneath
The eye, as the roads telling you

How the rain tattles on everything
It touches. The pavement has no way
Of knowing the future leading

Into the valley. The wood of burning
Barnyards and bones, ash coughed out
And covering, gaunt and haunted,

Quiver of rhetoric. Oh, the weight of it,
Possible as grief and hesitation,
As blindness and the wind-struck structures,

Edged and peripheral mustache,
Part fastened fashion, part flag or shadow
Of the flag on this hysterical country.

COFFIN FOR HEAD OF STATE

a pecha kucha after Fela Kuti

[DOG EAT DOG (Instrumental)]

Inside the coffin was a tomb. Inside the mouth of the bull-
horn was a tomb. Inside the stems of the violets: tombs.
Inside the thin blue shawl of the afternoon and of the dusk.
Inside the words *awe, freedom, territory, fatigue*.

[WITCHCRAFT]

In one village I came to a woman shaped like a bird
and was given a knife as long as a feather. In another
a woman spit a curse to break me like an egg, its sweetness
running between my fingers like something the body makes.

[BEASTS OF NO NATION]

I was born in the year of the war between wars.
I was born to a religion I thought could not hold me
ransom, to sermons walking on the back of the wind.
I was pulled from death's pocket and cradled in its hand.

[YELLOW FEVER]

My father was the sunlight now, but I couldn't understand
a word he sang. When his teeth were removed
and tossed glittering along the tracks of the trains,
I was quiet as the indicted. I myself was the music I lacked.

[GENTLEMAN]

In each village when I tried to tell them I was an American,
AmenAmenAmenAmenAmen spilled like ash from my mouth,
and they knew what it meant. Everywhere I was made
to dance like a man carrying his head before they cast me out.

[ROFOROFO FIGHT]

To be holy. To be united. To be untied. Could I ask or answer you,
I would be three things at once, I said to the coffin. To be uneyed,
unheavied, and alive, I said. To be the light on all the disappearing.
Words. To be burning and washed away. To be lit inside.

[ZOMBIE]

I walked, I walked, I walked. I was not noble, heroic,
compassionate holding the shadow of a name in the world.
I'd seen the scalp scorched by the way things used to be.
Including the smoke rising from the mind like a wing.
Including the hair burned of its ability to dream.

[EGBE MI O (CARRY ME)]

I carried a child's imagination, the uses of money,
the philosophies of grace, the paradoxes of revenge.
I carried a prayer book with words as small as the screws
in the glasses of the blind. I carried bad bad bad bad
badbadbadbad things, and the weight made my teeth ache.

[IKOYI BLINDNESS]

For Jesus Christ Our Lord. For the Grace of Almighty Lord.
For the wound and the bitter spit of the accused,
for the scar resting against my wrist for the rest of my life.
Because what I feared was in me was in me,
I wanted to lie still in the body like a knife.

[WATER NO GET ENEMY]

What I liked about its weight was what I liked about the sky
as red at the beginning of the day as it was at the end.
The gravity that was guilt or history. The darkness
that was smoke or cloud. The burning that was washed away.

[J'EHIN, J'EHIN (CHOP TEETH, CHOP TEETH)]

In one village vultures clapped their beaks at me;
they clapped their wings like the silly flags of providence
twisting against themselves. The body was soft,
the body was what I bore, the body was what I ate.

[NO AGREEMENT PART 2]

Inside the red of a feeling and irrevocably so. Inside the blood,
inside the yolk which is a warning. Inside the ghosts,
the field of oaths and conviction, the contracts of the state
going to business and busying the breath,
the eyes basked in the aesthetics of blindness.

[MISTER FOLLOW FOLLOW]

I almost described the leaves shining on their bones
and the snakes roosting in their sheaths to the coffin.
And the valley where all the headstones were smoldering.
But there was nothing left to be said, so I said it again and again.

[SHUFFERING AND SHMILING PART 2]

I carried it on my back like a man with one wing.
I carried it against my chest like a door with no housing.
With the blood which was its contrition. With the iron
which was its name. With the hunger which was its belonging.

[TROUBLE SLEEP]

I was born with my fingers on the latch of a coffin
hot with the sunlight spilling upon its face, locked
like a window in a building on fire. For Jesus Christ
Our Lord or against him. For the Grace of the Almighty.

[ORIGINAL SUFFER HEAD]

My coffin the moth house, my coffin with no message
or lover. My coffin cooled by stars spilling on its face.
My coffin the mouth. My body could have fit inside its body
and drifted downstream to the center of the earth.

[SHAKARA]

After my mother sang the only hymn she knew,
she tore her black dress open the way one tears
a scab from its address, and I saw the skinny knife
she kept hidden between her breasts.

[EVERYTHING SCATTER]

I am not in the village filled with prophets. I am feeling
elegiac for our cataclysms, the blood in the yolk
when the egg breaks, the grief stripped of its shell.
I am filled with the hollowness of holiness and breath.

[YE YE DE SMELL]

I am the inside the village reddened by readiness.
Inside the word *tear* and *tear* and *fatigue*. Inside
the terror which makes territory evaporate.
Where the sunlight braiding my scalp is on my mind.

[COFFIN FOR HEAD OF STATE]

He dead yeah nownownownownow, the villagers sang,
when I tried to tell them I was alive.
He dead yeah nownownownownow, the villagers sang,
as I carried my coffin toward them. *He dead yeah
nownownow,* the villagers sang, as I carried it away.

[COCKTAILS WITH ORPHEUS]

BULLETHEAD FOR EARTHELL

I don't know what the soul mutters
in the moment before the slang
of gunshots, sweat jeweling
the brow, braggadocio jumping
from the skin, blood thrusting out
a feverish gasp, the wish for nothing
worth holding between the hands
turned up to Heaven, but I know
if it happens, you must be my grandfather
at the moment of an ambush one
morning in Vietnam's Ia Drang Valley.
Because in the moment before death
none of the moments before that,
I know, bear the same risks.
A naked towel turned up to Heaven
on the bed with the same sprawl
of softness as the woman upon it, I realize
in the moment preceding the moment
of death, does not represent the moment
of death. It could be the broth of a spasm,
the fever of gasping, the moment of death.
It could be the fitful woman holding you
to earth as the seed leaves your body.
Even a boy with no father carries in him
the image of his father. And it must be abstract
as dream, pure theory, the moment of death.
If you are good, and even if you are not good,
the bullet enters the blood like the bony finger
of the god who put it there, and the future
scampers down to cover you. Granddaddy,
when my father, the first time I met him,

tried to recall your face, there was nothing
but smoke coaxing our history from his breath.

SUPPORT THE TROOPS!

I'm sorry I will not be able to support any soldiers
at this time. I have a family and a house with slanting floors.

There is a merciless dampness in the basement,
a broken toilet, and several of the windows are painted shut.

I do not pretend my dread is anything like the dread
of men at war. Had I smaller feet, I would have gladly enlisted

myself. In fact, I come from a long line of military men.
My grandfather died heroically in 1965, though his medals have been

lost. I try to serve my country by killing houseflies. I am fully
aware of their usefulness, especially in matters of decay.
Napoleon's surgeon general, Baron Dominique Larrey,

reported during France's 1829 campaign
in Syria that certain species of fly only consumed

what was already dead and had a positive effect on wounds.
I bet when my grandfather was found,

his corpse shimmered in maggots, free of disease. As you can
tell, I know a little something about civilization.

I realize that when you said "freedom," you were talking
about the meat we kill for, the head of the enemy leaking

in the bushes, how all of it makes peace possible.
Without firearms I know most violence would be impractical.

I thank you, nonetheless, for mentioning how soldiers
exist to defend my way of life. I am sure

any one of them would be an excellent guardian of my
house. I admit I have no capacity for rifles or gadgetry.

I cannot use rulers accurately. I realize
the common fly, like the soldier, is what makes us civilized.

And I admit my awe looking on the marine with a talent
for making the eagle tattooed across his back rear its talons.

I realize were it not for the sacrifices of these young boys,
America would no longer have its source

of power. I have given considerable thought to your
offer, but I simply am unable to offer my support.

WHATEVER HAPPENED TO THE FINE YOUNG CANNIBALS?

I would eat you, were it not for the pain
of my big tooth wiggling like one of those small doors
cut into doors so that pets, small dogs mostly,
can come and go as they please. What I have eaten of you
tastes like mint and damp clay, tastes exactly like the soil
I ate in my grandmother's yard as a boy. They called
me savage then, because I reeked and wreaked havoc
on the slim flowers so well acquainted with the sun.
A dwarf could fit inside this door in my head and steal
every thought you've furnished. You say
I should never comb my hair, and it's precisely why
my mother fears you. For house pets being American
is a cinch. For house pets being American is a guilt-
free luxury. Even when the bed is damp, the bedsheets
dizzy with lovemaking, I won't brush my teeth.
And when the smell is impossible, I will remember my
brief career as an infant. And then I will remember calling you
from a phone booth beside a cow field on the eve of war.
The dwarf burns the house down, and I myself am mistaken
for fire. I would bite you. I would battle the specter of death
until YOU LOSE hovers on-screen in a bloodshot arcade.
I would eat the hot light spilling from the west.
I would eat even the birds I don't trust, the rats with wings.
What's up, homeboy? you say, all fray-colored and mythy.
I am thin as nothing I have a word for. Full of dissonance
and dwarfs decreeing rumors. Full of rancor and dissidence.
I was saying *Feed me* before you smoked the last cigarette.
Before you smelled of the contentment that is not a food at all.

IMAGINARY WEDDING SONG

You can never be a bride for more than a day
unless you are the bride of Moose County.
Or bride of the Sea Island Fair. Or the bride of altitudes.
Or the bride of scrimmages. Or the bride of a miner's
lantern. The bride of eaves or the easy bride of naves.
The bride of the Second Avenue Glory Bound
Greater Covenant of Holiness in Christ Chapel
or bride of the Rock of Ages Full Gospel Sweet Home
House of Prayer. The bride of blistering scriptures.
The young bride of Doctor Roland Fumes, the pastor.
Or the bride of anchored earlobes and slapstick lipstick.
Bride of the affirmative girdle and transparent mantle.

You can never be a bride for more than a year
unless you are the bride of a flamboyant boy king,
princessed and pressed in something as white
as luxury. Or the bride of withering edicts.
Or the bride of John Shore's windup contraptions.
Or the bride of Abraham Jones, the butcher.
The bride of Delfeyo Nekrumah and his handsome
handmade spears. Or the bride of Yukio Imaura
and the fish. The bride of James James Junior,
the eponymous. Or the bride of Wole Curtis, the masseur.
The bride a mile from the graveyard and the warmth
of good money. The bride of birthright hugging the finger.

You can never be a bride forever unless you are the bride
having control over death. Or the bride of the very last number.
The bride of communion on a pink sliver of tongue or the bride
of crucifixion on a slithery strap. The briefly new bride.
The bride of confections and sand in the mouth

of each pearl-studded slipper and sand in the mouth too,
lodged and gristling behind each rice-colored tooth.
The bride of vows that cannot be chewed.
The bride of falling water. The bride of spit in the sink
and spit on the mirror. A spoon brooding in the brew bride,
an onion stewing in the stew. The bored and tarnished bride
of a corset undone by what's due and what "I do" makes you.

LIGHTHEAD'S GUIDE TO PARENTING

To say there has not been a daughter born to my clan
for more than four generations is a truth almost as absolute
as the one about the speed at which the rain will fall

on this day a year from now. What's more, none
of the children born to my clan in the last century

had a father to slump black and whipped as blackness
on a big couch and say, *Come darlings, unstring my boots.*
Remember when we believed everything the future told us?

Therefore, I suggest corporal punishment as a way
to establish the boundaries between youth and adulthood;

between you and your daughter. Do not hide or guard
the cheese and crackers or ask if she understands truly
the meaning of understanding. The moon, she notes, is God's

nail clipping. Tell her, "Yes, you know nothing of Jesus
on the cross. Jesus at the crossroads. Jesus of the cross-

over, drive, and dunk: the team wins by one."
"You don't know nothing, the belt ain't taught you." Say that.
Remember when we were young enough to remember?

Remember when we believed everything evening told us?
It had been raining and then it wasn't. There was a damp quiet

resting on the lapels of the maples and the daylily's
monkish, which is to say *idle,* upturned face.
When you demand your child turn down the radio,

the only answer should be silence. If you are disciplined
with your discipline, he or she will love you

as he or she will someday love God, the theory goes.
When the darkness begins to really get dark, it will burn.
That's not to say life is without its degree of jazz.

The rain might scat were it not for the sunlight.
The light might solo were it not for the rain.
And everything in that kind of compromise could be absolute.

GHAZAL-HEAD

You no-good fork sucker, that's what.
You no-good backscratcher, that's what.

A blue thumbnail. An old light fixture. A toylike hammer.
A glass or tumbler. Bend your fingers, that's what.

You're one of those sleepers. Those pod people
Poking their noses, those nose blowers, that's what.

I could care less for your deluxe vacuum.
Suck your own luck, you no-good Hoover, that's what.

Gulp, gulp, I yelled at sunset when I saw it walking
Across the room like a no-good rumor, that's what.

No-count number. Indentured fender. Household cleanser.
Black-shoe cadaver. Beer belly dancer, that's what.

And I know you know I know and could care less.
Them ailments into amens; angst into anger, that's what.

Slow down, I told the boy with the knife.
Give me a hug, I told that mother hugger, that's what.

I lied, what about it? I loitered too. Like dust.
I did what you did like a no-good mirror, that's what.

What about it, po' mouth? You no-good goody-goody.
What about it? I know what I said. Lover, that's what.

I AM A BIRD NOW

When Antony a man like Nina
With a shook note corned in his quiver

Dolls a wig of light the way a wounded
Head is dolled and the song slung

From his grimace is no longer part
Of the body but shares some of its

History you know how I feel / the raw
Drawl drawn from the bottom of the throat

The hunger broken by what can and cannot
Heal in the much too dark to see

After the vase is asleep with the taste
Of the bit flower its moodiness and lust

You know how I feel / submerged
In a clouded jar altered and alert

The mind light-headed and hawked
Run-down and cloaked in awkwardness

You know what I sorrow when I lay
On your back Beloved and our lovemaking

With your back to me is a form
Of departure / you know how I feel

Terrestrial as a marriage like a wing
When it is no longer part of the body

Slung from a horn carved of metal
Slickened to shine a phrase winding coil

and the winded valves the song which aches
As it opens and aches as it shutters down

COCKTAILS WITH ORPHEUS

After dark, the bar full of women part of me loves—the part that stood
naked outside the window of Miss Geneva, recent divorcée who owned
a gun (O Miss Geneva, where are you now?)—Orpheus says she did

not perish, she was not turned to ash in the brutal light, she found
a good job, she made good money, she had her own insurance and
a house, she was a decent wife. I know decent lives in the word

descent. The bar noise makes a kind of silence. When Orpheus hands
me his sunglasses, I see how fire changes everything. In the mind
I am behind a woman whose skirt is hiked above her hips, as bound

as touch permits, saying don't forget me when I become the liquid
out of which names are born, salt-milk, milk-sweet, and animal-made.

I want to be human above the body, uprooted and right, a fold
of pleas released, but I am a black wound, what's left of the deed.

ARBOR FOR BUTCH

a pecha kucha after Martin Puryear

[VESSEL]

I am with my newborn son and the man blood says is my father
in a shit motel, and if each of us is, as I sometimes believe,
the room we inhabit, he is a bed used until it's stained.
Even if I knew this first meeting was our last, I would
have nothing to offer beyond the life I have made without him.

[THICKET]

In the far south where history shades everything,
there are people who fear trees. I once heard an old man say
I may be black as a crow, but I'm white inside.
Nowhere else does the sky do what the sky does there,
where the graves are filled with dirt the color of fire.

[RAWHIDE CONE]

We drank whiskey until we were drunk as the couple in the photo
my mother gave me to show him, the boy and girl swaying
at the edge of my future. I watched my father curl on the bed
like a leaf drained of its greening as my child cried
the way rain cries when it is changed to steam.

[BOWER]

Because I believe the tree is a symbol of everything,
one of us was the bough reaching across the road as fumes
scorch its leaves. One of us was a door opening and closing
in the darkness, one of us was a boat being carried downstream.

[MAROON]

My father and I sat in a motel room beside a highway,
where his pickup was the shade of a bruise beneath the glow
of the vacancy sign. Where he and his talk began
to evaporate. We were two fathers watching the faces
of two sons where the evening passed as it arrived.

[LADDER FOR BOOKER T. WASHINGTON]

Where the rain comes, long-toed and crushing the high grass,
swamping the land; where a slave talked his children
out of running away with the bottom of his shoe.
This is what it means to believe in ascension and fear climbing.

[SANCTUARY]

In the far south where sap jewels the bark, the teeth
of the saws are sticky and bittersweet. But I wanted to carve
a door out of the wood, and around that door I wanted
to build a room, because I knew what my mother wished for
and I knew from far off what she would need.

[C.F.A.O.]

The arm of the boy falls around the girl heavy as a branch
in the photograph with the gloss that's been rubbed
clean and the blurred inscription which nearly delivers
its message before vanishing. I drove the long night
to see the face my son and I wear like a mask.

[SELF]

Where history can be a downpour of joy or guilt spilling
its wrongheaded desire all over the body. Where
a boy and girl fought in a motel bed to make me, one desire
beating against another. Where my mother seemed to blur
calling him her first lover even after she said she was raped.

[BELIEVER]

In the far south my father, the first time I met him
said "God made nothing sweeter than pussy." We smoked
our history, we drank to our future until each of us was
a head of steam, clouds above each other's dreams.

[DOWAGER]

Where the plan was when I saw him to cut off his hands.
Where because of this man my mother would want me
dead, would want no limbs to branch inside her,
no cluster of sound waiting in a drum. Where
she wanted to, but could not shape her want into an ax.

[DEADEYE]

Sometimes my body is a guitar, a hole waiting in wood, wires
trembling to sleep. To identify what you are, to be loved by what
you identify, I thought, *This is how the blood sings into the self.*
I thought what was hollow in me would be shaped into music.

[BIG AND LITTLE SAME]

The first time I met my father I believed I would understand
the line connecting me to him, because a man rooted to his kin
can never be a slave. But he was like the road, skid-marked
and distant, like the rain breaking above ground and beating into it.

[SOME TALES]

In the far south where as one man swung from the limb
of a tree, he said, *I may be as black as this bark,
but my heart is light.* Where even when your lantern burns
out, they say the flame lasts. Where everyone I know
is ablaze with this story and darkened by its ash.

[RELIQUARY]

Certain arrangements must be made
if you want access to the past. With his room
without rooms and his truck without gas,
my father was a nail bent in the shaft of a hammer,
a wound the length of a kiss, a mouth bled of its power.

[CIRCUMBENT]

I am with the ones the blood says are mine, and if each of us is
as I sometimes believe, little more than a bray of nostalgia,
we are like the village mule chained to its muling. My father
fit a slim, ragged hand over the head of my newborn son
and said he sounds like a white child crying like that.

[MALEDICTION]

What if blackness is a fad? Dear Negritude, I live as you live,
waiting to be better than I am. Before sleep last night I thought
how it would be to awaken with all the colors of this world
turned inside out. And that was the name of my suffering.

[BASK]

The story my father told me did not reveal one body inside
another, the arms of the boy who would become my father
embracing the girl who would become my mother; it did not hold
the sentence rooted to the beginning of my life.

[OLD MOLE]

I am not doing anything now, except waiting like the bird
who uses the bones and feathers of other birds to build
its nest. I am on my bed of leaves thinking about the past,
how my father dragged his shadow across the room
the way a storm drags its rain.

[CONFESSIONAL]

Where there were too many trees and too many names
etched into the trunks; where the knots in the wood
were the scars of old limbs; where, to be reborn, the birch pine
must be set aflame; where the door if I opened it might have
revealed the lovemaking or abuse still waiting to be named.

MULE HOUR

Ma and me ride a blue mule into the South, where cockroaches
dream of the apocalypse and weep each sunrise bright as grief.
And crushed, their insides are milky as moonlight banked in cloud.
Because between nightfall and morning, the roaches crawl all over
Dominion in their secondhand shoes making deals with the angel
of exile, who does not call the Lord his master and is nobody's slave.
I'd like to call him, Father, the one wearing a vest of woven snakes,
but he will not answer, not in the storm which darkens our route,
not with the roach he keeps trapped in his mouth. Ma and me ride
a blue mule until its dumb heart gives out. She grips its tail and I
its ears and we drag it to the side of the road like a bag of garbage
on trash day, its muscles soft as cushion and its bones soft too,
like coil gone lazy in a couch, and we leave him burning with all
the humanity fire strips away. A blue stench rides Ma and me
deep into a dream of the South where the roaches weep
like the mules of slaves, where they are quiet as cows waiting
for slaughter, and if their backs shine like jewels in the field,
the roaches on parade, it's because they are bright in the rain
and filled with a wonder which cuts through them and the fields
they wander and the hands that pluck them from tobacco leaves
with the certainty of a blade. I want to live as the roach lives, without
a head or body, free on both sides of the grave, like my father
beneath a black umbrella spitting on the Lord before he walks away.

AIRHEAD

I. TRANSLATION OF A SCENE FROM A NONEXISTENT MOVIE

"You are just stupid,
cruel, and jealous,"
the emperor tells the prophet
just after the prophet says,
"Let me tell you what will be
the trouble with you,"
but just before
the emperor removes
the prophet's head,
which is to say, just before
he orders it removed.

II. SCENE DELETED UNDER THE EMPEROR'S ORDER

"There is no death beyond
the theory of death,"
the prophet tells the emperor
just after the emperor asks
for his head and just before
the head of the prophet
taking leave of body
can be heard saying,
"I have no form because
I have no allegiance
to form."

Notes

Several poems in this book are based on the structure of the *pecha kucha*, a Japanese business presentation format wherein a presenter narrates or riffs on twenty images connected to a single theme for twenty seconds at a time. The words *pecha kucha* are a Japanese adaptation/loanword of the word *picture*, pronounced in three syllables, like "pe-chak-cha." "Arbor for Butch," which is most faithful to the form, uses the wood sculptures of the artist Martin Puryear. Googling the section titles will provide images of the sculptures. Other poems inspired by the form use music ("Coffin for Head of State" uses twenty Fela Kuti songs), elements of fiction ("For Brothers of the Dragon"), and conversational fragments ("Twenty Measures of Chitchat"). For more info, go to www.pecha-kucha.org.

"Lighthead's Guide to the Galaxy" alludes to a line from *The Hitchhiker's Guide to the Galaxy:* "Ask a glass of water."

"The Golden Shovel" is, as the end words suggest, after Gwendolyn Brooks's "We Real Cool."

"The Last Train to Africa" is after Elizabeth Alexander's poem "Ladders." Like the form used in "The Golden Shovel," the end words come from her poem.

Elizabeth "Libba" Cotten, the musician mentioned in "New Folk," was a self-taught blues and folk singer and guitarist.

"Mystic Bounce" shares its title with a song on Madlib's album *Blue Note Remixed.*

The title "God Is an American" comes from a line in David Bowie's song "I'm Afraid of Americans," from his album *Earthling.*

"Snow for Wallace Stevens" references Wallace Stevens's poems "A High-Toned Old Christian Woman" and "Like Decorations in a Nigger Cemetery."

"Music to Interrogate By" shares its title with Jan Jelinek's "Music to Interrogate By," from his album *La Nouvelle Pauvreté.*

"I Am a Bird Now" shares its title with Antony & the Johnsons' album, *I Am a Bird Now.*

About the Author

Terrance Hayes's most recent poetry collection, *Wind in a Box* (Penguin, 2006), was named one of the best one hundred books of 2006 by *Publishers Weekly*. His other books of poetry are *Hip Logic* (Penguin, 2002), which won the National Poetry Series Open Competition and was a finalist for the Los Angeles Times Book Award, and *Muscular Music* (Carnegie Mellon University Press, 2005; Tia Chucha Press, 1999), which won the Kate Tufts Discovery Award. His honors include a Pushcart Prize, three Best American Poetry selections, a Whiting Writers Award, a National Endowment for the Arts Fellowship, and a Guggenheim Fellowship. He is a professor of creative writing at Carnegie Mellon University and lives with his family in Pittsburgh, Pennsylvania.

JOHN ASHBERY
Selected Poems
*Self-Portrait in a Convex
    Mirror*

TED BERRIGAN
The Sonnets

JOE BONOMO
Installations

PHILIP BOOTH
Selves

JIM CARROLL
*Fear of Dreaming:
    The Selected Poems*
Living at the Movies
Void of Course

**ALISON HAWTHORNE
DEMING**
Genius Loci
Rope

CARL DENNIS
*New and Selected Poems
    1974–2004*
Practical Gods
Ranking the Wishes
Unknown Friends

DIANE DI PRIMA
Loba

STUART DISCHELL
Backwards Days
Dig Safe

STEPHEN DOBYNS
*Velocities: New and
    Selected Poems, 1966–
    1992*

EDWARD DORN
*Way More West: New and
    Selected Poems*

AMY GERSTLER
Crown of Weeds: Poems
Dearest Creature
Ghost Girl
Medicine
Nerve Storm

EUGENE GLORIA
*Drivers at the Short-Time
    Motel*
Hoodlum Birds

DEBORA GREGER
*Desert Fathers, Uranium
    Daughters*
God
Men, Women, and Ghosts
Western Art

TERRANCE HAYES
Hip Logic
Lighthead
Wind in a Box

ROBERT HUNTER
Sentinel and Other Poems

MARY KARR
Viper Rum

WILLIAM KECKLER
Sanskrit of the Body

JACK KEROUAC
Book of Sketches
Book of Blues
Book of Haikus

JOANNA KLINK
Circadian

JOANNE KYGER
As Ever: Selected Poems

ANN LAUTERBACH
Hum
*If In Time: Selected Poems,
    1975–2000*
On a Stair
Or to Begin Again

CORINNE LEE
PYX

PHILLIS LEVIN
May Day
Mercury

WILLIAM LOGAN
Macbeth in Venice
Strange Flesh
The Whispering Gallery

ADRIAN MATEJKA
Mixology

MICHAEL MCCLURE
*Huge Dreams: San
    Francisco and Beat
    Poems*

DAVID MELTZER
*David's Copy: The Selected
    Poems of David Meltzer*

CAROL MUSKE
An Octave above Thunder
Red Trousseau

ALICE NOTLEY
The Descent of Alette
Disobedience
In the Pines
Mysteries of Small Houses

LAWRENCE RAAB
The History of Forgetting
*Visible Signs: New and
    Selected Poems*

BARBARA RAS
The Last Skin
One Hidden Stuff

PATTIANN ROGERS
Generations
Wayfare

WILLIAM STOBB
Nervous Systems

TRYFON TOLIDES
*An Almost Pure Empty
    Walking*

ANNE WALDMAN
Kill or Cure
Manatee/Humanity
*Structure of the World
    Compared to a Bubble*

JAMES WELCH
Riding the Earthboy 40

PHILIP WHALEN
Overtime: Selected Poems

ROBERT WRIGLEY
*Earthly Meditations: New
    and Selected Poems*
Lives of the Animals
Reign of Snakes

MARK YAKICH
*The Importance of Peeling
    Potatoes in Ukraine*
*Unrelated Individuals
    Forming a Group
    Waiting to Cross*

JOHN YAU
Borrowed Love Poems
Paradiso Diaspora